Secondary Silence

By

Virginia Johnson

Book Detail Stuff

Cover

Anytime Author Promotions

Proof Editing

Shelby West

This book is a work of fiction. People, places, events, and situations are the product of the author's imagination. Any resemblances to actual persons, living or dead, or historical events, is purely coincidental.

© October 2017 by Virginia Johnson

ALL RIGHTS RESERVED

No part of this book shall be reproduced, stored in a retrieval system, or transmitted by any means, electronic, mechanical, photocopying, recording, or otherwise, without the prior written permission of the copyright holder.

ISBN-13:
978-1978132153

ISBN-10:
1978132158

Table of Contents

Book Detail Stuff

Dedication

A Definition Tease

Prologue

Chapter One

Chapter Two

Chapter Three

Chapter Four

Chapter Five

Chapter Six

Chapter Seven

Chapter Eight

Chapter Nine

Chapter Ten

Chapter Eleven

Chapter Twelve

Chapter Thirteen

Chapter Fourteen

Chapter Fifteen

Dedication

This book is dedicated to the people that ensured it would get done.

My amazing PA, Janneke and the beta team!

Y'all kicked my ass through this.

A Definition Tease

Blood

noun: the red liquid that circulates in the arteries and veins of humans and other vertebrate animals, carrying oxygen to and carbon dioxide from the tissues of the body

Electromagnetic energy

noun: a form of energy that is reflected or emitted from objects in the form of electrical and magnetic waves that can travel through space

Prologue

Ashley

When sight is unseen, there is a moment of clarity that is lost to the darkened void. Trust and deception become risks that one must make in order to survive the chaos of the night. To be the trusted one, there is a level of responsibility that you must consider sacred. The truths that you are meant to keep are the difference between life and death. I am not at risk of death, or life for that matter being the ones that I have sworn to protect, keep me a secret as I do them.

Death is not quick. It is a slow and painful process designed to make moving on easier to deal with. The higher powers at hand make damn sure that you are sent in the right direction, even if it means crushing your dreams as they decide your fate. As the soul begs to stay connected to the body, you are left to fight for life in heaven or hell; or so we are taught. I have learned that there are eternal fates worse than hell. The Devil may reign in the apparent underworld, but the real monsters live next door.

Good girls go to heaven and sinners descend to be tortured by Satan," I repeated to myself as my soul refused to move on. I could feel myself being both torn from my existence, yet anchored to the same realm.

The pain was momentary as I slipped away, just far enough to dull the fiery burn to my flesh. My heart stopped pounding erratically against my chest as I accepted the inevitable death to my body. Fear raced through me while I realized that everything I had been taught was a lie.

We are able to accept death in the form of reward if we lived by the way of the bible. Unfortunately, people like me don't move on, we don't get to be judged. All of the good that was done as a human is void as I am forced to begin a new life as a stranger to my friends and nothing more than a ball of energy to the more sensitive.

Everyone has a future; a reason for life. The task of "doing the right thing" is relative to the person that defines "the right thing." I was gifted an asshole with entitlement. My deciding angel made it clear that I would serve another purpose on Earth. My time was up as the person that I was and I would now be the person that I had to be. Good or bad – there was nothing stopping me from doing the right thing.

As time passed, I became more and more convinced that I had been forgotten and my hope for everlasting eternity crumbled at the door of the only person to accept me for what I was; a girl with nothing to live for with an ability that had gone untapped. My future held more than wandering the earth as a peasant while living the life that I couldn't avoid... until now.

Chapter One
Ashley

Without warning, I am thrusted in to a vision only meant for me. Duty calls.

"Will this be all for you, sir?" The petite clerk asks the next in line as she reaches for a plastic bag. One item at a time, the bag fills with random snacks and drinks.

The man responds with a stiff nod that goes unnoticed by the girl but not me. Watching closely, his eyes flicker back and forth between the window and the door. The empty gas pumps show no sign of immediate use, as the man otherwise, stands perfectly still waiting for his total.

Behind him, a younger guy rounds the gum rack, stopping directly behind the first. His eyes are unmoving; unblinking. Tattoos peek out of the top of his t-shirt as he fidgets with the bottle of water in his hand.

The first guy doesn't make eye contact with the girl as he hands her the cash and walks out without his change.

"Sir..." the clerk tries to stop him, but he quickly disregards her attempt.

The second guy pays for his bottle of water and leaves, turning in the opposite direction as the first.

Like a movie on repeat, the scene replays, again.

The clerk greets. The first guy sees something outside that is obviously fucking with him. The second guy leaves.

Repetitive dialogue and moments caught in time are what I am left with. There has to be something that I am missing, I thought as I closed my eyes and started it over for the hundredth time. *The girl, the guy, the guy, the empty parking lot, blood.*

My eyes shoot open as the end suddenly changes. The delicate girl behind the counter was tied to the ceiling by her own tendons and veins that had been pulled from her wrists. The bloody ropes were that of her own body. The blonde ponytail that she had delicately tied back, was used as a noose as it was tightly wrapped around her neck. Her eyes, void of sight, were removed from the sockets leaving a hollow grey mass of dying muscle and flesh.

Crimson drops fell from her mutilated arms as the remaining heartbeats ceased to push the blood from her open wounds. The spatter pattern was... missing. There should be blood, something more for me to focus on. It was as if this vision was designed for me. If that was the case, I know exactly who was responsible for it.

"Dammit, Thaddeus! You son of a bitch." I fought the urge to scream, but the thoughts couldn't be contained. "Get out of my head!"

My eyes shot open to find a very humored Thaddeus standing in the doorway. His dark hair hangs in his eyes as a smile crosses his face. If I didn't know any better, I'd think that he didn't want me to figure out who these guys were or what was happening in that convenience store.

"Sorry, Ashley. I couldn't help myself. You were taking yourself way too seriously." He leaned against the door frame as he spoke.

I threw myself against the bed as I stared at the ceiling in hopes that he would disappear. "Is this real, or am I chasing a ghost?"

"You are a ghost, it would only make sense that you would try to catch them," he said as he pushed himself from the door. "On a serious note, did you see anything that I didn't"

"No, Thad. Unless the blood bag that was suspended from the fluorescents was a normal occurrence?"

"Come on. There is only so much *vision* that I can take without having a little craving." He winked as I rolled my eyes.

His cravings were the worst for my visions. I saw the things that he couldn't see but when he fucked with me, there was no way for me to focus. Working for a vampire was no small task especially since he couldn't trust anyone but me. I swore to help him ever since he found me. I was born sensitive to the other side and I died to serve them. I hadn't moved on and I was at peace with that future. When I met Thaddeus, he showed me the potential for good that I could do for him. He was the first and only person to ever see me, if you can call it that. He ensured that I would be his for as long as he was *alive*.

"The first guy was waiting for something. I don't know what he was watching for but there was definitely something outside those doors that had him on edge." Giving him my opinion was always accepted and never wrong.

"I'll let you be. If anything changes, let me know. I need to find someone with a pulse if I am going to put up with you much longer," he said as he smiled and left the room.

I always expect him to mess with me and he knows how I feel about his *feedings*, but they are a necessity for his survival.

After he left me to my own movie time, I took my chances that he had stopped influencing the facts. There was something in the parking lot and it was my job to figure out who or what it was. With unnecessary deep breaths, I closed my eyes and focused, this time I put myself at a different angle. I watched from the closest gas pump as the first guy approached the register.

Inside the store, I had already memorized their actions. I watched lips move as I followed the timeline, knowing the missing information was outside based on the flickering eyes of the first guy. Scanning the lot, I saw nothing out of the normal. Trees swayed with the breeze, the street lights flickered and the bats flew high above... nothing.

I saw nothing. Nothing more than what everyone else sees in the dark. Pacing back and forth in front of the store, I refused to blink as I waited for the store to clear out. Guy one, left his change with the clerk and he pushed through the door taking a sharp left. I could hear her yelling for him with no response. So far so good, nothing has changed from what I saw the first hundred times I replayed this.

What I didn't see, what could not go unseen, was the way his body thrashed against the brick wall. What looked like the climax of a horror movie, was my dark reality and there was nothing I could do about it. Blood was the only thing left against the brick while the ground pooled with falling intestines and organs that weren't meant to be exposed. His body moved through the air, folding itself in half as I watched his soul step away from the scene and fade to dust. The only problem was that I couldn't tell Thad who it was that was attacking him. I wanted to, but there was no way I could.

The attacker was... me.

Chapter Two
Ashley

I am an undead being, leaving me with no reason to be passed out on the floor like a frat boy on a Sunday morning. I have been this way for a long time and I have never experienced the visions as I have over the last week. Finding out that I was responsible for the attack at the gas station has taken its toll on me.

Thaddeus continues to ask about the scene but I am quick to tell him that there is nothing that relates to the events. Nothing has changed from the order of events, it all ends the same. I am always the reason for the death of a seemingly innocent man.

I can't help but think that maybe he was on his way home to his kids with the bag of random snacks. Maybe his pregnant wife was patiently waiting for him to return with her midnight craving. *Ugh.*

I can't do this anymore and constant focus has led me down a rabbit hole of emotional turmoil. I want for nothing more than to return to the life that I once had. I was a good person, did the right things and always looked out for others. The fire was an accident that I couldn't escape. Having fought like hell to get out of my house, I waited for the fire truck to come and save me. The movies make it look so hopeful as the fireman races in to the raging flames that lick at the boots of the hero while he saves the girl. I can assure you that the movies are wrong.

"Is there anything else?" Thad pulls me from the memory of my loss.

"Nothing more than an hour ago. Are you going to tell me more about what I am looking for? It would help." I start to plead with him for something more to use to avoid my own guilt.

"You know that I can't tell you what I know. I need you to be focused on what you see, not what I have been told." His steps are heavy as he passes me on the floor. "This has never taken so long before. Is something wrong?"

My need to please him is fighting with the necessity to know the truth, "I don't know what to tell you, I am doing everything the same."

"Alright then." He seems upset by my response, but I am not sure that I am ready to explain it all to him, yet. He placed his hand near mine as he sat down on the bed. I crawled from the floor to the bed next to him and felt an overwhelming need to see something else. The adrenaline that was surging through me may have been anxiety but I was ready for something; something different than the man in black.

"Is there anything else that I can see? I need a distraction, Thad."

Before he can answer, everything goes black. At first, I am convinced that I passed out again but I can hear his voice within my thoughts. His whispers immediately calm me down and allow my mind to open up to his mental influence.

The front seat of the car is littered with fast food bags and beer cans. The driver belches while wrapping his dirty fingers around the pint of whiskey resting between his thighs. His inability to decipher the difference between the gas and the brakes were obviously alcohol induced. I watched as he slammed the bottle against his brittle teeth as I waited for one to chip. The steady stream of liquor from the corner of his mouth fell to his lap as the muscles in his face neglected to respond any longer.

Through the slurred lyrics poorly sung from his diaphragm they were causing my face to twitch and focus even more on the scenery outside of the vehicle. I couldn't continue to watch the double yellow lines swerve below the death trap he was driving. I was getting nauseous while encased within the car. The smell of the man's breath caused bile to rise, threatening to fill my mouth. I haven't had this experience since I was alive.

Trees rushed by as the speed increased. The world passed at such a fast pace that I never saw the other car coming. The man veered off to the left, smashing in to the front end of a passing mini-van. The car came to an abrupt halt, locking the seatbelt in to place. The driver was pinned between the steering wheel and a car seat.

Tears filled my lower lid as I realized the severity of the crash. Time stood still before it moved in fast forward. Before I could move to help the baby locked in to the car seat, the engine of the car burst in to flames. I was frozen in place as the history of my past repeats itself. A man and woman stand off to the side with two small children wrapped within their arms. Pointing to the engulfed car, the woman tried to run to the car seat with the man securing her wrist, preventing her from moving any closer.

I felt for the woman as she watched the body of the baby cremate itself on top of the burning hood of a drunk driver. The blackened smoke made it impossible to see what was happening but I certainly tried and there was no way the baby was surviving. If Thaddeus gave me this vision to see, there had to be a reason and I didn't want to let him down, again.

"Ashley, are you okay?" Thad's voice could be heard through the screams from the family. "Ashley!"

The concern in his voice pulled me back from the hell that I was witnessing. "I am here. Sorry, that was not an easy one to see."

"What are you talking about? I didn't have a chance to give you a vision," he admitted, worrying me and my sanity.

"I saw the drunk guy, the crash, the family; I didn't make that up. I saw it all and it was real."

"Maybe you need to take a break," he started to say.

"Maybe you need to shut the fuck up and let me do what I do. If you didn't send me that vision then who did?" I may not have intended for it to sound as harsh as it came out, but he needed to know how I felt. *I just told a vampire to shut the fuck up, I must be losing my mind.*

His laughter filled the room as he sat down without touching me, "You have been working on this for weeks and you are surprised that you are seeing things? Ashley, what you need to do is read a book or take a walk through the garden. This isn't doing you any favors."

He was right and I was not willing to admit it, yet.

"I will take a break when I figure this out, okay?"

"I have some things to do over the next few days, will you promise me that you will not work yourself in to a coma? I kinda need you." His eyes softened with his tone.

"I am not going anywhere. If you get out of my room, now, I will go for a walk. Does that work for you, boss?" I said sarcastically.

He stood, turning towards me, "Don't get yourself saved while I am gone." With that, he walked away, leaving me to my horrific vision and no desire to see it again.

There was no reason for any of them to die. The blood and the fire was all too much for me. The memories of my existence prior to

Thad, were kept suppressed for good reason. Maybe he was right, I need to get out of this room. The garden was everything that I had ever dreamed of while I lived in the city; beautiful and mine. I was unable to plant the flower beds, due to my transparent condition, but Thad followed directions and gave me a place to go when I needed to relax.

There are things that I was told I would forget in time, but I want to make sure that there is beauty keeping me grounded to the real me. The person that I saw ripping apart an innocent man was enough to make me never want to fall in to the trap of sin and sorrow. I watched as a man burned to death as I had. The fate that I was given could be considered a gift, since Thad easily could've turned out to be a monster like the rest of the blood thirsty scum in this city.

I have only encountered a few of his kind while Thad entertains. The parties and the smell of iron permeates the air as you'd expect from the home of a vampire. Following one of his welcoming events, I was forced to endure the mass quantities of blood, thirsted for and digested in whatever way it was consumed. I do not venture out past the gate. I could leave if I wanted to tour the area and risk being seen by a random stranger with the same gift that I had been given but there is safety in not knowing.

I play it safe, I always have, that is why these visions are so out of the norm.

As I pass the row of lilac bushes planted near the back of the garden, I pass my hand through the violet colored petals that match the color of Thad's eyes. There has to be more to the nightmares that I am enduring, but finding the link is going to be a real pain in the ass.

"Ashley, I have to go. There should be no visitors and the gate will be locked. If anyone shows up, they don't belong here. Stay away from them, do you understand me?" He says as he maneuvers through the garden as I wait for him to come to me.

Vampires are weakened by the sun, rather than bursting in to flames. That was one of my first questions for him when I found out what he was. Back to the movies and all of the shit that we are told as kids, I was shocked at what I thought I had knew and the false safety that the sun provided. I didn't believe in vampires, but I saw spirits, leaving me with some sort of reality that included one of everything.

"Are you listening to me?"

"Yeah, I'll be fine. I haven't left yet, why would I?" I reminded him as I compared his eyes to the lilacs, again.

He shakes his head as he kneels to pick a few stray weeds from the path. Something is bothering him and it drives me crazy when he doesn't talk to me about it, but it's usually for the best.

"I shouldn't be long. A few days at most." He tosses the failed flowers in to the bucket at the back of the garden.

"What's the big deal? You have left before and everything has been fine. What makes this trip so different?" I had to ask. He was hiding something and I didn't like the way he was acting. I mean, I was hiding something and I assumed I was acting just fine.

"Just be careful. If something doesn't feel right, it isn't, okay?"

He was starting to scare me with the cryptic message that he was trying to hide from me. I wanted to ask more questions but that would've been pointless because he wasn't going to tell me and I was smart enough to know that.

"Okay. I'll be here when you get back." I felt the need to reassure him that I was not going to disappear overnight.

A smile crossed his face as he ran his fingers through his hair. Beneath his lips I could see his fangs begin to extend. It didn't happen often and I wasn't afraid of them anymore, but there was more to this occurrence. They only make an appearance when he is hungry, horny or ready to fight. Asking which of the three was bothering him would never get me the answer that I wanted, so I didn't even humor the question.

With a deep breath and a second glance in my direction, he quickly made his way down the row of mums.

"I certainly hope so..." he whispered as he left me alone in the garden.

"Ah..." I stopped myself as I had heard him question my loyalty. I was his and he knew that I couldn't leave. Now, he thinks that I would pack up and run without notice. Whatever he was thinking, I was going to prove him wrong. I will be here when he gets back and I will have the answers that he needs from the visions even if I have to admit it was me causing the massacre.

Chapter Three
Ashley

The gazebo is the perfect place to disappear in to my own personal hell. If I was going to find clarity, I need to be in the right mindset. As I pass through the screened door, I feel my nerves begin to calm. White sectional sofas line the perimeter of the glass encased haven. Small end tables decorated with fresh flowers grow from the terracotta pots that I had picked out to match the throw pillows and flooring.

The rising sun glows through the aged stained-glass ceiling, casting abstract reflections of blue, red and yellow. Having lost the ability to feel temperature changes, I remember frosty winter days and the warm summer nights. The rainbow color rays dancing across the room helped me forget about the reasons that I am out here in the first place. What I really needed to do was focus on the fact that I was causing death in an unforeseen past, present or future. The problem is that there is no way for me to know what I am looking at without Thad force feeding them to me. The only thing he has seen is the convenience store clerk; the one I mutilated as I watched helplessly. Having had the car accident vision without force, I knew I had to start there.

Getting comfortable, well as comfortable as a ghost can get, I decide the couch would be the normal thing to do even though it really didn't matter. The memory of the soft foam below me was enough for me as I closed my eyes and hoped for the best.

As my nightmare flashes behind my lids, the flames continued to taunt the sky with the yellow tips of their end. I watched as the blue burned the hottest from the base of the fire. Trying to drown out the screaming family, I closed my eyes and listened for anything to clear my conscience. As it stood, right now, I just killed a man and a baby while I sat on the side of the road content with my actions. I don't give a fuck who I think I am, I deserve a fate worse than hell for killing a baby.

I had to clear the tears from my cheeks as I tried to forget about the body count and more about the surroundings. Focus, Ashley.

Having nothing to go off of, I was left to see whatever was thrown at me. I normally have direction, a part of the story, this time I have nothing. I shouldn't say nothing, I have a drunk driver. Before I could stop it, the vision went dark and I blinked back to the driver pouring the caramel liquid down his throat. I was watching and reliving the crash again.

Maybe this wasn't the intention that I had, going in to the sequence, but maybe I could see what I had missed. I knew I was going to be dizzy while he recklessly crossed the yellow line. He raced past the moving vehicles on the right as I watched and focused on the man. Waiting for the family van to come closer moved in slow motion. I saw the look on the dad's face before I saw anything else. Mom was reaching back to the little boys in the back, readjusting the strap on one of their belts. I refused to look them in the eyes. I needed to separate myself from the humanity of the situation.

The car seat kept my attention as the drunk fuck turned hard to the left. I closed my eyes and embraced the impact. Again, I find myself on the side of the road with the family, breaking a little piece of my heart off each and every time I look to the burning engine. Why does this have to be real? Why can't this be easy?

I could feel myself start to wake up as the darkness pulls me deeper.

80's rock booms from the oversized amps lining the stage. There was a cover band, fit with the long Van Halen hair and marker for eyeliner dancing across the front of a slew of screaming women. The girls reached for the stars as they hoped for the chance to be let back stage to meet their rock gods.

Having never had a life as a teenager, I wondered what it would be like to meet some of the greats of my time. They weren't as flamboyant as the ones entertaining the female libido, but I now wonder if I would've felt the same way.

There was nothing abnormal about this situation. Concert, music, food, beer and a lot of screaming fans made the ambiance of rock and roll real. As much as I wanted to sit back and enjoy the guitar riffs blaring through the speakers, there was a reason that I was here and thank fuck, here were no children.

The lead singer was kneeling down in front of a teary-eyed fan as the music slowed and the lights dimmed. It wasn't exactly the best music for my reason to be here knowing someone was going to die, but the moistened vagina in the room was a telling sign of the love song I was to expect.

Having done it before, the harmonic voices echoed through the room only causing the girls to scream louder. The whispers of forever and the promise of love was enough to make these women pools of hormones. I wasn't sure what I was waiting for but I sure as hell hoped it was almost over.

The crashing bodies jarred the stage causing a cymbal to fall from the drummer's ensemble. The bass player rushed over to fix the drum set by placing the stand on the raised platform. Not a single note was missed as the high notes were hit and the girls went crazy. I watched as they fought for the attention of the band or the guards.

Without warning the stage buckled, sending the lead singer in to a rolling spin towards the end of the stage. As he tried to catch his footing, a spotlight snapped above him, sending it crashing in to the dry ice strategically placed at the front of the band. Without anything to grasp on to, he flung his arms around, trying to avoid the fire that was starting to flicker.

There was no way to prevent the sudden flicker of the lights throughout the venue as the breakers started to reset and the women began to scream. The smell of singed hair permeated the area leaving the only thing left of the man they had all come to see. The scent of death and rotting flesh.

My eyes flew open as I watched the man fight to stay in this world. There was no way he made it although the girls begged for it to not be true. The repulsive stench that permeated my nose was enough to make me gag. I was dead, yet he smelled so god awful.

"What in the fuck was that?" I said as I sat up on the cushions. I grabbed the nearest potted plant, breathing deep the intoxicating floral aroma in hopes of clearing the man from my insides. "Ugh." I could only imagine my body decomposing like old meat on a hot summer day but I liked to think it was exactly the way I chose to remember it. Dressed in my red sequence dress, ready for the night of my life while I paired it with a pair of strappy heels. My blonde hair pulled into a messy bun, yet curled to perfection. There was nothing like dressing up with nowhere to go. I miss my life but I am happy with the after-life. Well, I was happy with the after-life.

Fucking Focus, Ash.

Accepting that there was no way to escape the singed carcass or the smell of fresh death, I needed to go back in. Returning to the same place on the couch, I make a cross over my chest, as I had as a human, and hoped for the best. This one was not as bad as the others I have been haunted with, leaving me less freaked out. What I didn't see coming was what I was met with when I closed my eyes.

Virginia Johnson

Chapter Four

Ashley

It was too late. I was too late. The sun had set as I regain my footing within the gazebo. Falling would do no harm, but the human side of me refuses to let me become anything else.

Without a plea to the wind, I start through the darkness of the garden as I wait for Thaddeus to return. There was only so much that I could do and I wasn't sure where he was going. I only hoped to God that he didn't see what I just did.

Only once had I projected a memory to Thad. He was strong enough to send them to me but I was weak in comparison. Only recently have I been able to syphon enough energy to tell him the time without words, much less share an entire...

"Ashley," I heard Thad's voice echo through the driveway as I stilled at the edge of the garden.

"What are you doing here?" Ironically, I stared at him as if I had seen a ghost. "You aren't supposed to be back for three days."

"I have been home for an hour, looking all over for *you*." Panic caused his forehead to wrinkle as his breathing slowed the closer he marched towards me.

"Why did you come home early?" I was still dumbfounded by his early arrival.

"What are you talking about? I left three days ago, now I am home."

Before he could say anymore, I lifted my hand to his face. There was no fucking way I was out for three whole days, was there?

"Are you okay, Ash?" I could feel him and the difference in his presence. The closer he came the stronger I felt; almost like an energy being passed from person to person. My fingers twitched as he reached for them. His hand stopped just short of my hand, dropping to his side in defeat.

"I saw it. I saw your vision. Why did you show that to me?" He looked as confused as I did in that moment.

"How do you know it was me? Maybe it was someone…"

"Cut the shit, Ashley. I know it was you. What I want to know is why and how, while you're at it." He wasn't budging.

"I don't know why. I laid down the night you left and I woke up just minutes ago. I was deep in a vision for three days, Thad. I don't know what is going on."

He ran his fingers through his hair before looking back to me, "How do you know the man from the vision?" Fear may have been something I felt as he asked.

"I have never seen him before and I don't think I ever want to. Do you know him?"

"Yeah, I know him and I plan on killing him if he ever comes near you," he said as he looked over his shoulder towards the shadows.

"Is he here?"

"No. He won't come here."

"If what I saw is correct, he certainly will come here. I just don't know how it ends," My words become whispers as I tried to push the feud from my memory.

As if to console me, Thad lifted his hands, as if to place them on my shoulder, "You are safe here. I have made sure of it. But as you saw, there is more to your fate than you may know. You saw the vision from your point of view, but I saw it from mine and you and your abilities run deeper than you can imagine. I need to figure out what it all means." He took a deep breath and turned to the house. "I hope you know that I won't let anyone hurt you, right?"

I do know that he would keep me safe. I know that he was incapable of letting me be placed in harm's way, but this was a different kind of war. This wasn't a kiddie fight on the playground. What I saw, was vampire royalty and the king was pissed.

"How am I different from any other ghost that is attached to a Vampire?" I needed to know the truth about my role in the future of his world.

"Do we have to do this now?"

Do we have to do this now? Is he serious?

"I just watched the ruins of the vampire empire unfold during a three-day nap. Now, you are telling me that there is more to my involvement than you are willing to share. I am done playing games and I am sick and tired of being roped around here with the weirdest dreams. Pardon me if I think I have earned at least a fucking lie!"

I could feel my anger starting to cloud my judgement. The closer he was to me, the stronger I felt. I couldn't explain it and I didn't know how else to deal with it. I wasn't going to sit here and listen to him go on and on about a future that pertains to me but is none of my business. Going inside sounded perfect as I followed him up the stairs. He pushed the door open and stepped to the side, as if I needed the fucking door opened for me. I was a damn ghost.

With anger on my shoulder and my pride on the floor, I didn't allow him to fully move out of the doorway before passing through him.

Before the pain filtered through my aura, I found myself breathless. Standing side by side, I reached up to Thaddeus out of instinct as his mouth hung open and the color drained from his face. I could feel the rush of warmth flow between us as I absorbed whatever he was giving. I couldn't move when he needed me to the most. I tried to pull away but it was too much. I was a ghost, I thrive on the energy of my surroundings but this was different. This was a shot of adrenaline straight in to the heart being delivered at Thad's expense. Before he hit his knees, he reached up with both hands and did something I haven't felt in decades; he pushed me.

I tripped over the entryway and fell to the floor. It wasn't the soft kind of fall that I normally experience; this was a fall to the hardwood. No passing through, no dramatic trip, not even a flicker to my feet. I felt the bruise on my arm begin to throb as my body scrambled to stand up. Supporting my own weight was involuntary and I was voluntarily having to learn how to do it before I made a fool out of myself, again.

"Ouch," I winced as I touched my skin. *I touched my own skin?* "What is going on, Thad? This has never happened. You have walked through me a hundred times; this shit has never happened before." I wasn't backing down nor was I walking away. He was going to talk if I had to kill him myself.

"You want to know what makes you so much more important than the others?" He stood, using the doorway to brace his weight. "You are one of the only ones left." He looked to the ground defeated and struggling to gain his strength. I could see that whatever I just did, I drained him of what was keeping him together.

"How? There were many of us. You told me that. Every vampire has a watcher, all of them." I was confused and rambling, surprised that he was still listening.

"Ashley, most of them did. This is a new world and the stake isn't for power within the Vampire royalty," he started as he gathered enough strength to stand up straight. "The weakness of every vampire is in the hands of their watcher. You are the reason that I am alive and I intend to keep you alive much longer than I. Now, can you not ever do that again, it hurt like hell." He made his way in to the kitchen as I stood, staring at the back of his head.

"That's it? I have enough energy flowing through me to produce skin and you want me to let it go?" I wanted to grab any large object and show him what he is dealing with, but I know I would look like a fool trying to pick up anything at this point.

With a heavy sigh, he finally looked in to my eyes, "I have no idea how you did what you just did. To be honest, it would've killed any other ghost. Let's not do that again, okay?"

Well, fuck. If it's going to kill me, "Yeah, let's not do that again," I had to agree.

Before I could leave the kitchen, Thad made his way through to the dining area and I immediately felt like myself again. The rush ran its course and I was thinning out, no longer in need of muscles that I haven't had in forever.

There were still unanswered questions and I wasn't getting anywhere with Thaddeus. If I was going to find the information that I needed, I was going to do it myself.

Chapter Five
Thaddeus

The bullshit myth that vampires don't sleep couldn't be farther from the truth. We sleep with the intention to renew our strength, although I have been sleeping to relieve it. Chasing the constant leads that threaten my livelihood and the only thing important to me, has created mass hysteria amongst the hierarchy; my hierarchy.

Ashley was never supposed to find out this way. I never wanted her to know that she was at risk of losing everything, again. Her first life was the fault of many, this one is mine to protect. I need her more than she needs me and it scares the hell out of me.

Kicking my shoes off, I want nothing more than to sleep a dreamless night. Everything I have shown her until now, has brought me closer to my goal. I will find him and I will end this.

The pillow softens as I lay back on my bed. The stucco ceiling reveals patterns within the texture. I watch as the patterns change with only one thing on my mind. Days grow old as time never ceases. My entire existence was nothing more than a feeding frenzy, a slaughter house full of empty veins and decay. Living for nothing more than my next fix was that of a newborn. Many say the phase in which a vampire turns to when a vampire regains their humanity lasts only a few years.

    I proved them wrong. I faltered in the systematic ways of the lore. My humanity evaded me for almost two centuries. Two hundred years I spent moving from city to city, wreaking havoc on unsuspecting victims that wandered down the wrong street at the wrong time.

    Pulling the pillow over my face, I try to repress the guilt that seeps from my skin as I remember the last person I wanted to kill; the one that got away. I was no different than a meth addict. Without a source, there is no threat but I was faced with the one thing that could make me crumble. The blood flowed through her veins as I watched the color drain from her face. I was nothing more than a monster in that moment and I was sated.

    Ashley changed me, but now I worried that it wasn't enough.

"Fuck this," I mumbled as I pulled myself to the edge of the bed, holding my head in my hands.

Thinking back to the run-in with Ashley, there is no reason for any of this. I have killed vampires before, out of necessity, and I have never become the one thing I wanted to destroy.

"Thad," Ashley's voice reminded me that she was still here and I had been doing the right thing.

"Hey." She stood in the hallway behind the closed door.

I could hear her hair slide through her fingers as she nervously chose her words.

"I guess, good night," she whispered without coming in to my room.

Did I want to continue a conversation with someone that sucked the life from me? There was no question, I did. Not tonight, though.

"Good night, Ashley."

Footsteps would not follow her movement as she disappeared. I could feel her as she moved away, leaving me to my own recluse. I can't lose her and I will make damn sure that no-one takes her from me.

I push my palms against my eyes in hopes that this is all a dream. It is my dream, my reality and I am not ready to give it up. She changed my life, I couldn't let her go, yet.

The lights dim as if they recognize me. Looking around, there is a room full of swollen arteries and flowing blood. Fifty-six beating hearts. Fifty-six reminders of my lifetime in hell. Fifty-six reasons why I should slaughter everyone in this church just to prove a point to the believers. Fifty-seven bodies. I am convinced that they don't believe I exist and the thought brings a smile to my face.

"Why are you smiling?" A young blonde stands next to me emotionless, staring straight ahead. Although, I couldn't see them her eyes locked on the rose-colored box being brought to the front of the room.

"I want to drain the life from everyone here; including you," I say, less for shock value and more because I fucking mean it. The smell of death was intoxicating.

She turns to look me as I look away, "Well, don't let me stop you."

Her footsteps are peaceful and elegant as she walks away from me. No-one walks away from me. Who the fuck does she think she is?

"Hey," my voice echoes off the walls and colored glass encasing the vaulted space. She doesn't stop moving, unlike the others attending the little gathering. I look over to an older man before pursuing her, "You should thank her," I say pointing to the bitter blonde standing near the front, "she may have just saved your life, old timer."

Leaving him to process that tid-bit of information, I watch as she stops only inches from the chrome detailed box, leaving me no choice but to stalk towards her. I can hear the whispers behind me as I pass. If they only knew the truth that I have no fucking idea why I am here. I saw a church and I walked in. Vampires are allowed in the church, as well. We sin the same as any other asshole asking for repentance, only we need more than a prayer for forgiveness.

The blonde stood front and center while all eyes were on me. She was the one I yelled at, yet I am the one they are gawking over?

"Did you hear me? I said I was going to..."

"Kill everyone in the room?" She never turned around to answer. She stood perfectly still as I stepped next to her. "Yeah, I heard you. I just don't care."

Silence filled the room as I tried to get her to look at me. This time I wanted to see her; I wanted to remember her. Her unblinking eyes were covered by wisps of hair, absent of any kind of emotion as she spit my intentions back at me. It was only then that I realized she was different.

"If you want to feast, start with the front row. They are only here for one reason and one reason alone; to look good. They never loved me. No-one did." She turned around to face the crowd of people that were staring directly at me.

The pastor, dressed in the full church garb, grabbed my elbow, "Sir, please take a seat. We are going to begin the service."

This guy has no idea who he is messing with. I have already planned on killing everyone in here and he is only speeding up the process.

My mouth opened but the words didn't come out; they couldn't. Behind my next meal was a picture, a sight that I will never forget. The most beautiful woman I had ever seen.

Her red lips grinned as she glanced towards the ground. Wavy, blonde hair danced behind her shoulders as she did the one thing that I don't remember doing. She was enjoying the moment. "I know her," I say to the pastor.

"Ashley Swan. Lovely girl." He reached over to the casket, placing one hand against the box and the other crossing his chest.

"I just saw her, she was standing right here." I pointed to the floor beside me. I want to turn away but I can't look away from the beauty in her picture.

"Son, she passed in a fire. She is with our savior, now. Please, have a seat."

I wasn't here to attend a fucking funeral. I was here to feast like the monster that I am. This girl was nothing more than an inconvenience to my plan. I grabbed the silver cross from her casket and anticipated my actions towards the judgmental sinners.

The church painted itself red as I turned to the weeping souls. Their blood pumped faster while they cried. I could smell the fear of death within their last breaths. The thoughts that passed through my mind were appetizing and horrific. Bleeding bodies mounted to the ceiling tiles as I walked through the thick crimson rain, drinking droplets as I passed beneath their stilling hearts. Feeding from the weak and fallen as the screams cease.

"Don't do that!" With the sun radiating behind her like a glowing angel, I lost my appetite. Standing at the door, under the archway of the church, rays of gold surrounded her while she begged me to stop. *"I saw it all. Please..."*

Staring in to her eyes, I looked back over my shoulder to the picture. The happiness that she had once felt was gone. Sorrow and pain was all that she had left for the people here and I didn't like it. The cross fell from my hand as I realized what she was doing here. I now know what I am doing here.

My legs moved on their own as I closed the gap between us, leaving the pastor and the grieving in my wake. When I was close enough for only her to hear me, I tried to explain, "Ashley, I am a dangerous..."

"Vampire?" She finished my sentence in a whispered tone.

"Yeah, vampire. I am not a good one, either. Not like the ones you see on TV or in the movies." I waited for her to either disappear or respond. I wanted to turn around, to take in her picture again, before she vanished. For the first time in a hundred years, I wanted to remember something, anything. I couldn't take my eyes off of her as she grinned and

looked to the floor, mirroring the vision I just had of her.

None of this made any fucking sense. One minute I want to slaughter a church full of funeral attendees, the next I want to help this girl that I had just met. I am losing my damn mind, since she is a fucking ghost. No wonder I was the only one that everyone was staring at, I was the only one here.

"I am a ghost, I take it?" *Her eyes looked up to me as if I had all the answers. That's when it hit me. That was the moment everything changed and I was no longer protecting only myself. She is meant to be mine.*

Great fucking timing.

"Yeah, you are a ghost. Unless, there is someone else that wants to crawl back in to the body in there." *I point towards the chapel.*

Her laugh was only heard by me, draining my body of the darkness that I carried for two hundred years. The corners of my mouth twitched as I nodded.

"I can handle you," *she said with a smirk.*

Then everything went black.

Virginia Johnson

Chapter Six
Ashley

I saw it all, everything he just relived through the memory of my funeral. There were missing pieces that only I could fill. The look on his face when he escaped the torture of his past, the immediate trust I had in a man that shouldn't be trusted and the day the color of his eyes changed. Black turned violet with the finality of his own perfect storm. Amethyst strands weaved their way through his iris, breathing a new life in to the murderous vampire that threatened to tear the throats from my family and friends.

My vampire.

Saying good night was my way of saying good bye, sadly. I was going to find the answers that he refused to give me. The last time I was outside of the gates of his home, I was leaving one life and starting another. Tonight, I would return to the danger of the outside world with little expectation of returning home. Preparing for the worst was the only thing stopping me from leaving without saying good bye.

Easily passing through the walls of the house made my escape easy. There was protection within the walls of his property, unlike the place I needed to go. Fear drove me to Thad, hope was taking me away.

Standing at the rod iron gate, I took an unnecessary deep breath and let my eyes close. It was now or never and I knew there was little time to break free from myself.

"I am coming with you," Thad's voice reverberated within the stone walls. "You are not leaving me."

Stilled and shocked, I didn't move. I waited for him to open the gates and pull the car up. The sleek black exterior matched the color of the midnight sky as I admired the beauty in something so simple.

"Are you going to get in?" Without the need to open the door, I took a hovering seat next to him.

"You don't have to do this."

He sighed as he pushed numbers on a keypad, illuminating the opening of the gate. I watched him as he finished setting the alarms on the house. I had no idea that there were so many security systems in place. He had to do this every time he left the house and I had no idea why?

"I do this for you and yes, I do have to do this."

Crossing the threshold of our home, I was going to start giving directions, but the roads are different. Buildings stood where there were none, businesses lined the streets and people went about their night as if we didn't exist.

Watching the trees pass by as we moved closer to the edge of town, Thad took a quick right down a dirt road. I wasn't familiar with anything any longer, so I was thankful for his navigation. Dirt roads turned to gravel and the forks forced us one way or another.

"I haven't been there in forever," I attempted to start a conversation while he accelerated and slowed down through the darkness of the night.

He didn't respond while I gazed out the window. When I opened my eyes, I was standing on the road, alone. There was no longer a car and no Thaddeus.

Laughter filled the empty void that the country acres provided. I rolled my eyes as I waited for the lesson to be taught. I was starting to accept the fact that these episodes were going to come whether I wanted them to or not, but I still didn't like what I saw when they hit.

Breaking through the trees was a handful of boys; six of them. They all pushed and hollered at each other as they moved along their path. All dressed in the local high school football jerseys and jeans, they trampled the wild flowers growing in the fields.

"Do it. It will be funny, man," one of the boys from the back jogged to the front, pointing to the leader's cell phone. The antagonizing didn't stop as they laughed about whatever they were encouraging. I waited and watched as they tripped over the metal bars buried along their path.

"Nah, he isn't worth it," the teen went to pocket his cell phone as the rumbling of the engine moved closer. The silence of the woods was inundated with a roar as a bright light began flickering through the trees.

"Our ride is here," one of the others spoke up as he tucked in his shirt. The group stopped and waited for the train to move closer while the leader opened his cell phone again.

Approaching at a faster speed than I had expected I watched the boys prepare to run alongside of the moving train cars. The boy on the phone was feverishly typing on his cell while his friends started yelling at hm.

Without responding, he grinned while his thumb hovered over the screen. I watched as he contemplated his next move, whatever that was going to be.

Train jumping was a sure way to die and I knew for a fact I was going to watch it all happen.

Before the young man could finish up on his phone, I watched as it fell from his hand followed by the torturous screams from his friends. Looking to his buddies, covered in blood splatter and bone fragments, I saw the glow of the screen illuminating the blades of grass where he once stood.

Two of the boys were frozen in place as the others wiped what remained of their friend from their skin. I pinched my eyes closed as I waited for it to repeat, as the last visions had. Balling my hands to my eyes, I hope the tears that threatened would subside until I knew what just happened. I had to focus and the empathy was too much. I just watched a teen lose his life to stupidity and reckless behavior.

"Do it..." My eyes fly open, not wanting to miss anything. As they make their way towards me, I decide to try and prevent it. I had to do something if I was going to watch the souls sucked from someone so young and new to life.

He stands still as he stares at his phone with the look of the devil in his eyes. Whatever he was looking at, there was no good to come from it. For a split second, I found myself not wanting to help him, but that isn't who I am nor what I was sent to do.

The train siren blared as the boys shouted the order to start running. The boy smirked as his thumb moved closer to the screen. In slow motion, his thumb print was threatening to send a message. I couldn't see what he was saying, but I recognized the colored bubbles filled with words.

Only millimeters from sending the message, an arm reached out, stealing my attention from the screen. The moment didn't last long enough for me to stop it. The arm that extended from nowhere, not only ended a life, but it belonged to me. Another me, but me all the same. I pushed the young man to his death. I did this.

His body wrapped around a metallic wheel before severing his corpse in to pieces. The carnage continued to multiply as each wheel, from each car, passed over the limbs and organs that were standing in front of me only moments before.

My mouth wouldn't close as I stood there, unable to do anything but watch as a mother would no longer say good night to her son, a friend would never receive another phone call from him, a football would go uncaught - all because of me.

I glance to the ground below at the blood coated screen, leaving few unsent words for me to see, "...miss you...be happy."

Those words would never be seen by the person that he missed. They would go unsaid to the one that needed happiness in their life, all because I ended it.

"Ashley, you are crying. What's wrong? Where did you go?" Thad ripped me from the emotional hell that was plaguing me. These are only getting worse as I see them. I grip my head, pushing hard on my temples in hopes that, I don't know, I can make them all go away.

"I am seeing shit. Things that I shouldn't because it isn't real. It feels real, but it isn't. It can't be," I say as he pulls through the gates of the place that I needed to be.

"Rivermore Cemetery," he says as I start to regret my decision to do this.

Virginia Johnson

Chapter Seven

Ashley

Statues line the driveway, protected by the rod iron fences that match the perimeter. Like houses, mausoleums fill the buried ground with families left all in one place. I was left alone and forgotten as I had always been. The car came to a stop along the gravel tire tracks. The engine quieted, leaving only the sounds of nature and death to fill my ears. Climbing from the seat, my eyes were focused on the stone angel, perched above the marble maker. I couldn't see what it said, but I knew it was mine.

Years after my passing, I had returned to my grave. Overgrowth covered the headstone as I made unlikely promises to myself; ones only a human could keep.

"What promises?" Thad whispered from over my shoulder without touching me. I wasn't ready for that again.

I turn to him as he shakes the flashlight to charge it, "I will never leave someone that I love..." I wasn't sure he would understand. He was a Vampire, a creature created to wander the world alone.

Without waiting for a response, he smirks and crouches down in front of the falling angel. The long grass and dandelions were yanked from the soil, leaving a clean edge, framing the timeline of my life:

Ashley Swan

December 18 1953 – January 18 1980

That was all there was left of me. After a tragic fire and a life with a vampire, this is all I was worth to my family, my friends; to anyone.

"You know that's not true," Thad says, trying to make me feel better. "The old timer at your death party looked like he missed you. Or, maybe he was happy that it wasn't his demise they were celebrating." His smirk made me laugh as he finished cleaning off the debris that I was incapable of pulling.

"Thank you."

"I'll be right over here, take your time," he looks like he wants to say more, but he stops himself before turning to a row of mausoleums. I watch him walk away from me as the loneliness seeps in. Not only am I creeped out by a graveyard, I am alo…"

"You're not alone," I hear Thad yell from the other side of the structures.

With a sigh, I kneel at my grave. Running my finger along the dark etchings, I focus on the reason for my being here. I palm a handful of dirt and slowly release it to my body, "for you are dust, and to dust you will return," I whisper to the ground, reminding myself that there has always been a path for me.

I remember the little things about my life, the good things. Murder and secrets were foreign and it was killing me to think that I was keeping anything from Thad. He was my better half, even though he had done much worse than I.

Stop thinking about it, he can hear you. My inner intelligence spoke up in time for Thad to join me. His steps were heavier and his breathing was more labored, but he was here.

"Well, well, well. What do we have here?" The owner of the voice stood in front of me and it wasn't Thad.

I was frozen in place. I was invisible, yet a man with the darkest eyes that I had ever seen was taking in my every feature as if I was real.

"Don't worry, babe. You are not crazy." He started walking around me like a cat stalking its prey. "I am curious though. Why would you be wandering free during the witches' hour?" He waited for me to respond but I was swallowing every word that threatened to escape. I only stared in to the eyes of a monster.

I was wrong, he wasn't a monster, he was much worse.

"Does it matter?" I was hoping to distract him long enough for Thad to realize something was wrong. He wasn't here and he wasn't coming. I tried to focus without avail. Words and thoughts evaded me as I stayed kneeling over my shard corpse. Well, hovering above the 6 feet of dirt covering what's left of my forgotten body.

Heavy steps began pacing alongside of my headstone. I watched the padding of his steps rather than the demonic look across his face. Darkness wrapped around the dirt as he rolled heel to toe in melodic tempo. Like fine mist, the aura mimicking his movements kept my attention drawn to the ground.

"Where is he?" The footsteps stopped and he turned towards me. Waiting for bravery to overshadow fear was becoming increasingly difficult. I wanted to scream at the highest decibels in hopes that someone would hear me. I was rendered speechless to the living and the undead. "I know that you know where he is. I can sense him, but he is not here to protect what's his?"

I can hear the smirk form across his face without looking right at him. The chills that I faced were directly linked to the beauty in his features and the aura that plagued him. I knew as soon as I looked up, there would be nothing more than a creature of vanity, prepared to attack and that was the moment that I realized I was in danger. Never before had I feared for my existence, or lack thereof. Thad's words replayed like a vision as I anticipated the worst. *"You are one of the only ones left."*

Scenarios flooded my mind as I stayed in place. I knew he was a vampire, I could sense him. What if he was the man that invaded my memories, the one that Thad swore would never come here? What if he kills me before my vampire can finish him off?

I wasn't ready to disappear, to be captured by the same kind of monster that I swore to protect. I was stupid to come here and even worse off without Thad.

Now, I had to respond. Open my mouth and actually convince him that I wasn't worth it. What was I going to say? *"I have no idea.*

Haven't seen him in a few minutes so maybe he is on his way to grab a latte?"

Acceptance of my fate beat the answers to my own questions. I rose from the ground, continuing to gaze at the only remaining parts of me; the pieces buried deep beneath the surface. There were no answers buried below the grass and dirt, they were standing in front of me.

I am a coward cloaked in defeat and I needed to remind myself that there is a reason for my being here. If he wanted me dead, he would've killed me. As I rolled my shoulders back, his heavy steps moved away from me. Darkness surrounded me and darkness was needed to keep Thad safe.

Out of habit, I filled my chest with a breath that I no longer needed and looked my stalker in the eyes. The words that I had planned to say were strangling my strength. The vampire standing in front of me is much more powerful than I had given him credit for. Violet eyes stared back at me as I tried to keep my strength intact. He began to circle me from a safe distance while I prepared for his attack.

"Who are you?" I asked in attempt to distract both of us for different reasons.

"Drake, but you won't need to know that. You know what I came for, I can sense it in your fear." He is right. I am afraid.

I am standing atop my grave as a ghost while I fear for my existence. He was everything that I would have been attracted to as a human; strong, confident and gorgeous. Had I needed air to survive, I would have passed out by now. There was no movement between us once he stopped only mere inches from me.

He looked as if he wanted to speak, mirroring my exact stature. As I grew in strength from the encounter, I noticed the color drain from his skin.

He is too close. He did this to himself.

I pull myself from the hypnotic state I fell in to, dragging my foot across the grass. As I had hoped, tension pulled at my foot. Thad was strong enough to be near me, this guy had a lot of power and I was draining him of it as he stood paralyzed in front of me.

As I squeezed my eyes shut, I could feel the wrinkles form at the outer crease. If what Thad said is true, this was hurting him more than it was going to hurt me, considering I was trying to stay upright. A battle of power, danced between us as he fought to hang on to what little life I hadn't taken. I tried to control it and give it back but I was quenching a thirst I didn't know I had.

As quickly as I had craved his energy, I wanted it to escape. The horrible things that caused him to acquire such darkness was too draining for my soul. As I stared in to his lowering violet eyes his body begins to fall, I remembered a memorable quote from the bible, a verse that explains everything, as I accept my punishment for this mistake.

Chapter Eight
Thaddeus

"No wonder, for even Satan disguises himself as an angel of light," her voice was weak as she finally let me in.

I have heard that verse; I am that verse, she just doesn't know it yet.

Without thought or hesitation, I race to her. Any other night, I would believe that she wouldn't leave without me, but after the actions that brought us here in the first place, I can't be so sure. I vowed to keep her safe and based on the Satan reference, she is head to head with a vampire. One that would rather see me dead than her suffer.

"Ashley," I thought, hoping to break through the wall she put up. I hadn't gone far, but it was further away than she needed me to be.

My heart beats erratically against my chest as I run to her. What feels like minutes, is only seconds. I spot her flowing, blonde hair only a few yards across from me, when she collapses to the ground next to Drake.

Before her head slams to the marble stone, I catch her. Surprised by the warmth of her skin against mine and the way her body falls slack in my arms, it reminds me of both the past and the present. Her solid form is breathtaking, yet I know it won't last.

For a moment, I am thankful that she absorbed Drake, because *that* pain was a bitch. He deserved to feel that soul sucking fury but I never want her to do that again. It could kill her and I am not going to let that happen, at least that is what I am trying to convince myself.

"Fuck," is all I could say as I watched Drake regain consciousness. I didn't want to leave Ashley, but I needed to make sure Drake knew never to try that shit again.

The way his body contorted in pain sated me as I gently placed her blonde hair across her own headstone. The color of her lips matched the color of the blood that I craved to see. There was no need to feed, only a desire to rip Drake's head from his fucking neck.

Standing to full height, I take small steps towards his weak body. I have no idea how long he will be down but I intend to make sure it isn't too soon.

"What are you doing here, Drake?" I can hear the wrath in my own voice.

With a deep moan, he turns towards me, "Fuck off. You know why I am here." He rolled over to his side to face me. "Why is she here?"

"She is none of your concern and you shouldn't be here. I want to know why you are."

His elbows rested on his bent knees as he worked to regain what little strength he could. Agony was the only way to describe the look on his face as the only person that I cared about lay unconscious, in human form, above her worldly corpse.

"Thad, there is something big happening. You are the only one left with," he was silent as he looked to Ashley. "You are the only one left with one of her."

What the fuck was he talking about? I was with a group of vampires only days ago. All of them were in possession of a seer as I was.

"They were lying to you. None of them have their help anymore. The collection has grown sparse for the vampires as the power within the lords has increased."

"You're here to see if I was lying as well," I said to Drake as he looked over to Ash.

"I certainly didn't expect... that." His head tilted towards the body as she stirred. I had never expected that, either.

"She is stronger than you think. She isn't going anywhere and I will make damn sure that none of you get this close again. Return to the assholes that sent you and deliver that message."

Kneeling beside her, I lift her in to my arms. Warm skin against mine is surreal as I stand, never taking my eyes off of Drake.

"Don't move," I instructed as I started to walk away. "I will kill you if you come anywhere near her."

His snicker made me halt in the damp grass. The fog was beginning to move in as if timed for effect. Before I could rip his spine from his neck, the threat became more vocal.

"I'll kill him, but first I'll make him suffer," Ashley said against my chest with closed eyes. Her limp arms wrapped themselves around my neck as I held her close.

"Ready to do that again, Drake?"

Without an answer, he was gone.

The ground was thick with moisture as the air cooled. The only thing I wanted to do was get her home. She was safe there and I could protect her from herself, if she was her only threat.

There was a violent part of me that wanted to go after Drake, removing him as a future issue. The big shots will know soon enough that she is still alive and what she is capable of. I have never seen a seer do what she did and I can imagine that it won't go through the rumor mill. There were only a handful of links that had yet to be severed and I wasn't letting her go without a fight; another fight.

Ashley stirred slightly as I made it to the car. Her dreams were increasing in power and the frequency was more than I had ever seen. The visions that I needed her to see were no longer an active part of her brain. She was seeing things from her perspective and I can't imagine it was her past or she wouldn't be here.

Holding her tighter, I pull the keys from my pocket to unlock the shadowed car. Thick fog seeped in to the car as I pulled open the door. Swirling in a tornado affect above the passenger seat, I watched the moisture dissipate.

With a heavy sigh and a final glance over my shoulder, I gently place Ashley in the car, pulling the seatbelt over her solid form. Knowing she is dead doesn't change the fact that I would take every precaution to keep her safe.

The echo of the closing door reverberates against the huge mausoleums lining the driveway. Planting both hands on the roof of the car, I look to the ground for answers. *I have no fucking idea what I am going to do next.*

Knowing that I need to make sure that she stays safe, there is no question that I barely know what is going on or how to stop it.

"How am I going to stop this?" I say to the darkness at my feet.

Pushing off the car I walk to the driver's side. Paying no attention to my surroundings, I get in the car beside her.

She looks peaceful, as if she were sleeping. Before I reach across to lay back the seat, I brush my fingers against her rosy cheek. With no painful power draw from me is both a good thing and a bad thing. The seat buzzes as it reclines, allowing her a little more comfort than she may need being she is filtering some pretty dark shit though her body.

My hand brushes against her arm, reveling in her warmth. Before I can move away, everything goes dark.

My eyes open in a wooded area at day break. The morning sun rays cast streams of yellow and gold through the branches. "This must be what it's like to be a movie vampire." The colors were abnormally bold and bright.

Scanning the area, I hear the familiar sound of a bullet aligning within the chamber. I don't see anyone around me, but this can't be good.

Heading in the direction of the unsettling sound, I break through the trees too late.

Standing over six feet tall is a large man wearing an orange vest, flannel shirt and jeans. His loaded shotgun is perched on his shoulder and ready to shoot. The blood flows quickly through his veins as I watch his neck pulsate with his heartbeat. The longer I stand there, more sweat drips from his fuzzy brow. *Fuck I'm thirsty.*

Time stood still while I stayed the hunger that was overpowering me. I couldn't close my eyes, though I was trying. Fixated on the warm, flowing crimson liquid beneath a layer of fat and flesh was not making it easy to avoid draining his oversized body of life.

My teeth dropped slowly from my gums. As I prepare to feast, the man wipes the beads of moisture from his forehead with his left arm, never lowering the gun. The irony in this situation was amusing. I am hunting a hunter.

Ready to take my first step towards dinner I heard her voice and stopped immediately.

"Don't do it," she whispered full of pain and sorrow.

Ashley stood behind me with a handgun raised and ready to shoot. I stepped to the side in time for the gunpowder to ignite, sending a spiraling bullet casing through the air.

Lucky for me, I stepped to the right. My prey wasn't as lucky. The bullet pierced the hunting vest, stilling the beating noise that had clouded my decision making. She shot a man in cold blood. Turning back to her, I watched as the tears flowed down her cheeks. She was becoming more and more empty as each droplet landed on the ground in front of her.

"I am so sorry. I had to do it," she cried as I abandoned the thirst that I couldn't fight before.

She was talking, but she wasn't talking to me. From the trees, a little girl dressed in a pink princess dress broke through carrying a crown and a picture book.

"Did you catch it, Daddy?" The excitement in her steps was replaced with terror as she ran towards the man that was bleeding from his chest. She couldn't be more than five years old. I wondered why he would take a little girl hunting, but to each their own. She didn't need to see this, no-one did.

Before I could stop the little princess, Ashley raced past me as if I wasn't there. I was here and I saw the whole damn thing. She just shot a man in cold blood and now she expects me to stand by and do nothing?

She stood over the little girl, taking her in to her arms, consoling her with, "shhh" and, "it will be ok," as I watched in confusion.

Without thought, I was moving towards the three of them. The picture book had fallen from the girl's hand, landing open to a picture of the man, the little girl and a beautiful woman, holding the little princess tight in her arms. They were all happy and smiling, unlike now.

"Come with me. I will make sure you are safe." Ashley stood with the little girl in her arms and walked away as if I wasn't standing there. She was ignoring me and it was fucking ridiculous. I just watched her kill a man in cold blood. Not just a man, but a father.

"Ashley," I yelled towards the duo as they disappeared through an opening in the trees. *Fuck this.*

Running after her, as soon as I pushed back the first branch there was a scream and a bright flash. With a quick blink, I was sitting in my car next to Ashley. She was panicked and breathing heavy. Looking out towards the darkness, I saw nothing moving within the shadows or the fog.

The engine roared to life as I raced to get home. Whatever the fuck just happened, I knew it wasn't real; it couldn't be. Ashley couldn't kill an innocent, she was incapable of it. It had to be a vision, one that I wasn't supposed to see.

Chapter Nine
Ashley

Awakening to screams, I saw nothing but darkness. It wasn't until Thad fiercely turned the key, illuminating the interior with a soft orange glow. The engine roared as he slammed the pedal to the floor. The headstones passed faster than I could handle.

"I killed him," my whisper was louder as a solid mass in comparison. He didn't say a word as the confession dripped off my tongue without its consent.

"You didn't kill anyone. That was nothing. Nothing more than a dream," he sounded like he was trying to convince himself of my hellish reality.

"Of course," I didn't know what else to say.

The car slammed to a stop in the middle of the road, "Look. I have killed people, Ash. I've watched a soul seep from the iris of a victim, that is something that you never want to see. Tell me that you haven't done it," he demanded.

"I have never killed someone...in real life." I didn't know how to answer that. I have watched myself kill many people; some over and over again. I know what it looks like, what it feels like to have your soul ripped from your body. That was the one thing that I didn't need to deal with right now.

"Why do I still have skin? Why am I real? I shouldn't be, I say trying to change the subject.

"Drake is a very strong vampire. There is no question that his, whatever the fuck that was, would let you... humanize for some time. Just don't do anything stupid with it," he sternly said without looking away from the road.

I stared out of the window, hoping that this *power* would wear off soon. I didn't want it. I could feel the darkness coat parts of me as it cycled through my body. I wanted to go back to Thad's house and pretend none of this ever happened. I don't want to fear touching the wrong person, especially Thad.

I have been through Hell and back without feeling like there was nothing to live for. Now, I am fighting that fight daily as I am constantly reminded of the bad things that I can do. I know it is just a dream, but what if it isn't?

An occasional car passed, slowing as they met Thad's black car on the road. The fog and mist grew thicker as the temperature dropped. Closing my eyes in hopes that this, too is a dream, I am disappointed every time as I open my eyes to the most uncomfortable situation I have been in during my afterlife.

My left-hand warms unexpectedly. Thad's fingers wrap around my hand, with a tight squeeze. His violet eyes darken as I stay as still as I can. The warmth is different than what Drake left me with. The cloud of fear dissipates as Thad's thumb rubs a small circle over mine. This is what being human is like, this is what I miss the most.

A connection with someone, someone that you...

Before I could finish, he rips his hand from mine. "I just wanted to check and see if it was wearing off." His eyes left mine and returned to the road, emotionless.

That is all it was? He was checking on me? I should've figured there was no reason for him to want to touch me. The last time, it could've killed him; I could've killed him.

"Is it?" I felt like I had to say something as I looked to my lap.

"You are still covered in him."

The way he said it, I felt disgusted. I had no control over the energy that I was trying to remove from my body. There was no question that I was nothing more than a ball of Drake to him. I looked to me, but I had the remnants of Drake coursing through my form.

"Pull over," I said.

"I am not pulling over here. We are in the middle of nowhere. We will be home soon. Then we will fix this."

I wanted out of this car as much as he hated being near me. He hadn't said it and he didn't need to. The look on his face said it all.

"Hurry. I want this over with."

Without another word from either of us, he sped through the country roads leading to the city.

The street lights were brighter and more frequent as we made our way through the neighborhoods. Time was endless as he huffed and puffed his way through the gates of his estate. I was thankful that I could be alone, yet pissed that I was the one that did this. It was my fault. If I would've just stayed home this wouldn't be a problem. The need to see myself, my resting place and my past caused more than I was ready to accept. Thad hated me, my grave was left untouched and I knew there was nothing good about being human. Humans have emotions and reactions that a ghost doesn't have. Emotions are one thing, but being human they are so much more debilitating. What I didn't count on was Drake.

"Just let me out," I couldn't look at him as I told him what I wanted. I wanted to be as far away from him as I could. He knew I was safe as long as I was in the compound that he barred me from leaving.

The car slowed faster than I expected causing my body to jerk forward against the seatbelt. Pain shot to my shoulder as he hit he latch, releasing me from restraint. With all of the emotions racing through me and the pain that would bruise if this was long term, I slam my body in to the door, trying to escape.

I stilled as I looked to the door handle. *Of course, you are a fucking body, Ashley.*

Pulling on the chrome handle, the door unlocks, filling the car with fresh air. I carefully stepped out, avoiding a fall that I didn't need. My balance was shot after tonight. How was I supposed to think much less walk?

Regardless, I needed to be alone.

"Don't go.."

"I won't," I replied as I started towards the garden. Blossoms were closed up for the night, leaving vines as the only thing I could focus on. My knees hit the dirt before I thought to do it. Pulling weeds from the flower bed was easier when I didn't need him to help me. Thad took care of the garden and always appeared to want to. I never had to admit that I needed him to keep the beauty alive. This didn't need me.

Feelings, human feelings are a real bitch to try to control. Right now, I struggled with one thing that I couldn't forget. I needed him. I wanted him, but maybe he doesn't need me. I need to go in the house, there was something that I have wanted to do for a long time.

Chapter Ten
Thaddeus

The only one left.

Drake's words won't leave me alone. There has to be more, otherwise Ashley is more of a target than I had ever imagined. Someone is collecting power, a real source of energy, for whatever reason they are forgetting that there are rules.

As much as I want to find the person responsible, I can't leave her alone. Not in her condition. She is different, right now. She has skin and color, things that I have yet to see from a seer. Ghosts don't have mass or warmth. She was warm to the touch when I reached for her hand. I fought like hell to avoid touching her, but in that minute, the one where the adrenaline wears off and reality crashes in to you like a bus, I realized that I could've lost her.

The fear of losing everything was worth it, if only to make sure she was there. I couldn't be sure after the vision I saw and the need to give up everything. The constant current of energy between us was for both assurance and possession. She is mine and Drake knows that.

I'll use the term loosely, but she was feeding off of him and it killed me to know someone else flowed through her body.

I couldn't sit in the car any longer. I had to burn off some of this anger before I took it out on her. She didn't deserve it but she was here.

The air was crisp as it hit my skin. I could hear music coming from the house as I walked to the empty garden. I thought for sure she would be here. I followed the sound in to the parlor, stopping without her seeing me. Her hands moved effortlessly against the grand piano as if she had been doing it her whole life. I never asked much about her past but playing piano was definitely on her list of pre-ghost hobbies. It had to be.

The sonata was recognizable but there were missing notes every few bars. I couldn't help but smile as I watched her skin fade and return as she played through the transition. She was returning to me without Drake poisoning her insides. I wanted Ashley back, my Ashley.

With a deep sigh, the music stopped. Silence filled the room following the loss of 'human' and the return of her ghost form. Her head hung as she stared at the keys in front of her. She wanted to keep playing and I wanted to make her forget Drake.

My footsteps were louder than I wanted them to be against the hardwood. She turned slowly, knowing it was me, and looked right in to my eyes. If a ghost could cry, this is what it would look like.

"I didn't know you played, but it was beautiful," I said as I sat next to her on the bench.

"Thank you. I miss the simple things," she admitted without looking away from me.

"Keep playing."

"I can't. I'm a ghost, remember?" Sounds of defeat hit me in a place that I haven't been affected in a very long time. I never wanted this and I wasn't willing to let it go. I had the desire to make her happy.

"Play," I instructed.

With a huff and an obvious distaste for my demand, she slammed her hands through the piano.

"Do it again. This time, don't try and hurt yourself," I chuckled to her.

Her transparent fingers extended and balled in to a fist repetitively. She wasn't in the mood to humor me, but I had to try.

At first there was nothing, no music, no happiness, but she didn't stop.

"Close your eyes, Ash."

She did as I asked, giving me a chance to help her even if it killed me.

I stood to her back as her fingers played a silent song. I wasn't sure what was going to happen to me, but I had to do this. I reached around her, placing my hands against hers. She stopped moving as soon as I touched her. The flow between us was quicker than I expected but she needed this.

"Keep playing."

I could feel her pull from me as if I was giving my life to her. I guess I was in a way, but there wasn't anything that I would rather do.

As her body began to return to skin. I pulled away without letting go. My body was telling me to stop but I refused. I gently held on to her wrist as she pushed down on a key.

"Don't do this," her gentle voice warned. "I can't do this without you."

"Then, play," I reminded her.

This time she didn't argue as I gently ran my fingers against her skin, careful not to lose focus or connection. One wrong move and she could kill me. In that moment she created music and I gave that to her.

"Ashley, don't be afraid. Trust me."

"I have seen what happens. I did it to you."

"This is different. I won't explain it, I want you to…" I was at a loss for words. I wanted to say things that I shouldn't and she started playing, leaving me in the clear.

Controlling my breathing and only allowing her to take so much was proving to be harder than I thought. I didn't know how much more I could give, but I wanted Drake out of her system as much as she needed to know that she can play anytime she wants.

"Thank you," she turned to me with a smile, separating me from her. This time I wasn't on the floor or suffering the excruciating pain. This time I was slightly weaker than I was, but I was willing to give that up for a chance to make her happy after all she has been through.

"You're welcome." I nodded and knew I had to get out of there. She really was beautiful but completely off limits. She was a ghost and

I, well I don't know what was breaking the rules anymore.

She was safe here and I needed her to stay that way until I could figure out how to end this before it was too late.

"I am going up stairs, I'll see you later." There was nothing more that I could say. I had work to do and for the first time, Ashley was a distraction.

She smiled as I walked away. My room felt empty as I walked in. There wasn't anything out of place, but I knew something was missing. Tossing my leather jacket to the chair, I grab a t-shirt and sweat pants. Needing a shower and a moment to get my strength back up, I pull my sweater over my head and turn on the water while I have a chance.

Looking at my reflection, I start planning my next move.

"Fuck. How am I going to figure out where to start?" I say to my own reflection.

Thin layers of steam begin to coat the mirror, leaving me talking to myself. I don't know what to do with her or the fucking vamp lords. These guys are up to something that requires enough energy to start real shit. A complete elimination of the seers is nothing any vampire would want, unless you are out to destroy your own kind.

"That's exactly what they are planning to do."

Slamming my hands on the porcelain countertop, the sink slightly pulled away from the wall. Without care, I hauled ass out of my room to the end of the hall.

I had no idea what I was going to say when I got there, but I needed Ashley to do her thing for me. It may be the last time that she is alive long enough to help, being she is one of a kind and she is mine. That alone puts her in harm's way at this point.

Stopping just shy of her oak door, I still. The intricate designs on the door made this a one-of-a-kind piece of wood, and it was perfect for her.

Struggling to find my voice, I held my fist inches from her door. I could hear her humming on the other side of the one thing protecting her from me.

She was singing the song that I helped her play on the piano. Rolling notes and key changes were pitch perfect and I was selfish enough to ruin this moment for her, or was I?

The best thing for her was to be as far away from me as possible. If the future that I expect collides with her, she will beg for something worse than death.

Chapter Eleven
Ashley

One moment.

One speck in time, changes everything.

There was nothing that I could do to stop him from leaving me in the parlor. I felt him disappear from my body as fast as he made the decision to leave. I had one of the best and worst nights of my after-life, and here I was, alone.

Drake felt like death as his toxic energy made a vile path through my body. Thad, on the other hand, he felt... amazing, like an April breeze in a cherry blossom field. Thad selflessly risked his own life to give me that moment.

Whether he knew it or not, he gave me something that I haven't had in a long time. He gave me back something that I loved and he shared that with me. One day, I would make it up to him, but until then I would do anything for him. He deserved me.

If it was too much to give me the strength that he should've kept for himself, he should've just told me. I should've stopped him, but the need to feel human was more important than his safety. Now, all I wanted to do was make sure he was okay. The pain in my happiness was hidden within the false sense of security he was giving me. Now, I needed to find him.

Thaddeus was responsible for every emotion that I was capable of expressing in this moment. Passing through the door, there was something that he was keeping from me and I was going to find out what it costed him to give me the strength to play the piano.

The hallway was eerily quiet and hollow. If fear had the normal response to my transparent body, the tiny hairs on my body would be dancing to the gods as a warning. Nothing felt right as I made it to his open door. The mahogany bed that I have seen so many times before, was untouched. The moisture from the shower drifted through the doorway as I slowly moved towards the room. He never would've left all of these doors open, even with my ability to walk through them.

The glass door was open and Thad was nowhere to be seen. Out of human habit, I looked tothe mirror as I let the loneliness melt away with the rolling clouds of steam as I entered the bedroom.

"Where are you, Thad?" I leaned forward on the porcelain counter top and everything went black.

Fluorescent lights flickered until the room brightened enough for me to see I was standing in a hospital room. The grey walls and sparse table tops were a telling sign that there were no visitors. Here I was, back in a vision and feared I would watch myself do bad things to good people.

The sheet hanging from the ceiling was pulled back by a nurse holding a syringe and an unmarked bottle. Annoying beeps were making it hard to concentrate and it didn't help that I was forced in to a dream that I didn't want instead of looking for Thad. The last time I slipped in, I was out for three days.

"The doctor will be in soon to check on you. Don't worry, everything will be fine once the IV gets to working," the nurse said to the guy in the bed. A teenager, at most, lie still, staring at the ceiling with empty eyes and a sole tear falling from his left eye.

Looking to the foot of the bed, I find the clipboard filled with notes and random scribbles that would only make sense to the medical staff.

From what I could tell, the seventeen-year old male took a fall and hasn't recovered from his injuries. Doesn't look like there was any brain injuries or spinal damage, but he was, by no means, responsive to any of the tests the doctors had tried. He was left in a room with nothing more than a few drab pictures and a television mounted to the wall.

Glancing to the boy, I think of the football game he is missing or prom that he will never dance at. First loves and life lessons have been taken from this young man with no empathy for the future he deserves.

As the nurse paces by the door with her eyes focused on her watch, she stops and looks to the bed and up to the monitors attached to him. The beeping becomes erratic, causing the lights to spike before they level out to a rhythm reminding me of a metronome. The steady bells give her permission to slip out the door unheard.

There has to be a reason that I am here and I needed to make it quick. As if I summoned the end of this dream, the teen flat-lined. No heartbeat, no movement and no reason for it. I ran to the monitor, trying to push all of the buttons. I am a fucking ghost with no way to stop this nightmare for happening. He was only a child and didn't need to have his life end this way.

I watched as I walked through the room. My reflection was standing on the other side of the bed in a less transparent form. I didn't see me as she, I, her, whoever she is, leaned down over what remains of a healthy body, mirroring me from the other side. She looks up to me with her finger pushed to her lips, "Shhhh."

The water in the shower has cooled, leaving no steam in the room and no sign of Thad. Beams of sunlight glow through the cracks in the curtains from the other side of the bedroom. Turning to the mirror directly in front of me, expecting to see myself, I see nothing.

"Thaddeus!" I scream from his bathroom. If I could cry, I would. If I could express any physical emotion, I would give all of this up.

Virginia Johnson

Chapter Twelve
Thaddeus

Stone bricks line the walls of either side of the hallway. Torchlights burn every few steps, illuminating my path to the dungeon of the Vampire Lords. I can't help but think this is stupid being the sun doesn't affect us the way the humans think it does. We don't burst in to flames or melt to the floor in a pile of ash every time a natural resource comes in contact with us.

This place would beg to differ, but fear of the unknown is a vice for feeding. The faster the blood pumps through the veins, the faster we are full. The human body has little control over the real threat to them. The monsters in the dark are a myth. Those of us that crave the consumption of your life source are hiding in plain sight, waiting for them to be in the right place at the right time.

"Thaddeus, we have been expecting you," the faceless voice echoes against the stone.

I shouldn't be surprised that they knew I was coming, only proving that I was right.

The future of our kind has changed and the Lords are responsible.

"Of course, you have," I respond without slowing my pace towards their chambers.

Locks turn as I move closer to the oversized double doors meant for me to enter. I haven't been this deep in to the caves in a hundred years. Not much has changed, aside from the smell of decay.

The heavy doors creak as they swing open, signaling me to enter. As I pass through the archway, the Victorian decorated room welcomes me with lighted candles and Drake.

Having recovered from his bout with Ashley, I can't help but grin. The suffrage that vampires wreck on humans is nothing compared to what Ashley was able to do.

"Where is your assassin?" I knew he was referring to Ash, but I wasn't going to give him the satisfaction of knowing where she was or that she was alone.

"She is safely away from you. Don't worry, your history won't repeat itself. Tonight, at least," I threaten.

"We know why you are here," a deep voice booms from behind me. I keep my eyes on Drake.

"Oh, please. Enlighten me."

Dressed in black, a man circles around me because I wouldn't turn to look at him. Taking his place between myself and Drake, he introduces himself, "My name is Christopher. I am nothing more than a vampire, like yourself." He extends his hand to me, welcoming a hand shake.

"I see no reason for these bullshit pleasantries. You have sent others for me and found what you were looking for. What I want to know is, why?"

His hands wrap amongst themselves as if he is applying lotion.

"Pardon me, but I know why you are here. Why don't we make this quick," he tucks his hands in to the pockets of his over-priced pants. "You have something that I need and you are going to give it to me."

With a chuckle, I raise an eyebrow to him, "I have something you want? What exactly is that?"

"Didn't Drake deliver my message as he was asked?" Christopher looks to Drake to ensure the act was completed.

"Drake? He delivered a message, all right. Was it before or after he was rendered unconscious by my seer?"

"About your seer, Thaddeus," he said as he started pacing back and forth for dramatic appeal.

My neck rolled uncontrollably in preparation for a battle that was eminent.

"Your seer has shown to be dangerous to our own kind and we are going to need to eradicate her from existence. You do understand, don't you?" Lack of compassion laced his words but there was something in his eye that told a different story.

"Are you kidding me? Our kind has been a danger to all seers. Consuming their energy and for what? For power, strength? I am not fooled by the loss of seers, but I'll be damned if you think I am going to hand her over to you." I left no option for negotiation because it wasn't going to happen.

"Thaddeus, it seems as if you have broken the rules. You know there are measures that we must take to ensure the safety of our system. You have been around long enough to know this, have you not?" He cocks his head to the side while asking the rhetorical question of the night.

"As you do, correct?" I respond, mocking his posture and the hypocritical shit that he is trying to force down my throat.

"I have done nothing to jeopardize our future, unlike your seer." Christopher turned to Drake, who was nodding his head in agreement.

"Drake had no business being here. He was looking for me and if I were given the chance, I'd let her do it all over again. Only this time, I'd let her kill him."

Christopher looked shocked by my statement. His head jerked quickly to face me with the mention of killing a vampire. Not just any vampire, but Drake.

"Your seer is capable of killing a vampire and you think there is nothing that we should do about this girl; this threat?"

"You really don't want to fight me. I am not in the mood and the last time I was here is the only reason you have a job. Remember, Christopher?" He is working my last nerve.

A smile crossed his face as he backed away slightly, his hands in the air in false surrender.

"Why yes, I do remember. You proved to be strong enough to syphon more energy from your own kind than any other. I, of course, blame your seer, but it made for a good show."

I couldn't stand still anymore. I could feel my tolerance for his stalling is wearing thin on me.

"Get to the point, Christopher,"

"The point is that you need to turn over your seer to Dominic. The less you fight, the easier it will be on her. It doesn't matter much, he will consume her and ensure the future of vampirism stays safe. Isn't that what you want?" I don't move an inch as he continues without my answer. "This is how it works, my dear friend. You will give her to us or we will kill you to get her. The choice is yours, Thaddeus."

There are too many things that still don't make sense. "With the eradication of all seers, that leaves us all vulnerable to an attack. This wouldn't protect us in any way, it would only put us at risk," I state as he stares over my shoulder.

"That is a risk that we are willing to take, so long as there is nothing anchoring vampires to their human life," he looks straight in to my eyes.

"I have been a vampire longer than most of you. I lost my human side a long time ago and you know I would never do anything to cause danger to my own kind."

I thought back to the day I found Ashley. Her fight for life had ceased but she wasn't willing to give up someone else's, even in the form of revenge. Her blonde hair, pulled in to a messy ponytail, even as a ghost. Watching her sleep through visions, walk through the garden and just hang out in my room, Christopher is right. I wouldn't take back the moment at the piano for anything, not even to save myself. I would protect her and destroy any vampire that tried to hurt what's mine.

Everything stilled as I remembered her pull of power. I knew what I needed to do and it was going to hurt like hell. It was worth it; she was worth it. I waited until Christopher was close enough for me to end this.

"You think you have any place in this conversation to argue? That, my friend, is not at all how this works," he said with certainty that I was willing to challenge.

"So, tell me how this is going to work? This is how I see it. You are going to leave Ashley alone and I am going to walk out of here without taking the energy you are permeating from all the seers that you have syphoned. I can see the orange flow through your veins and it looks quite painful, even for a Lord like yourself," It will hurt like hell, but I am willing to do it to keep Ash safe.

"You don't have the stamina to withstand my power. It would kill you,"

I didn't give him a chance to finish his rant as I slammed my fist in to his chest. Slowly, the undead was losing his will to fight as I felt the souls of seers attach themselves to my body. Burning from the inside, my muscled tightened as the strength grew. This was not the best idea but a necessary evil if I was going to save my girl.

"You'll never survive," Christopher croaked out as he struggled to keep what life he could. I was stronger than him and gaining more and more power with each and every ghost soul that I absorbed.

Their power differed as it attached itself to me, giving me everything that I wanted to avoid happening to Ashley. I couldn't take anymore as the strength turned to lava beneath my skin. Admitting to myself that this was the worst pain that I had ever felt, makes me wonder how he could control it.

Drake stood with his mouth watching as I stood to full height. Christopher's body fell limp against the marble flooring as I tore body parts from his chest.

Christopher's final breath was reassuring, as the crossover from his body to mine finished. I could barely stand, let alone function as I moved towards Drake.

"I am not the one that you want. Find Dominic; find your girl."

Before I could shred his body apart, piece by piece, I heard the angelic and damaging voice that owned me.

"No wonder, for even Satan disguises himself as an angel of light," I have heard her quote these words before, only this time she wasn't talking to Drake. *H*er broken tone was clear as day, filled with uncertainty and something stronger than fear. Wherever she was, she was truly afraid of someone; or something.

Chapter Thirteen

Ashley

I shouldn't have left. I shouldn't have left. That was the only thought I had as I entered the compound. The doors were of no difficulty since I could walk through them, it was the huge guard standing on the other side of it. He saw me as soon as I entered the stone lined corridor. Stilling and thinking my way out of this awful moment was of no use. I thought I had seen the devil in Drake, but I was wrong. This guy was everything that I should fear…and I did.

"No wonder, for even Satan disguises himself as an angel of light," my inner cry for help slipped and I hoped that Thad heard me. *Please hear me.*

"Lost?" He said, moving from the stool at the door.

The closer he moved, I could feel the pull to him. He was calling my soul away from my aura and I couldn't move away. His body glowed from the energy that he harbored. It matched the color of the sunset over a red sea of blood.

No, was all I could say while fighting to stay grounded to this reality.

"Ashley, I presume? We have been looking for you. I heard the rumors about how special you are. Drake was missing pieces of the night he met you, I am sure you could help fill in the..."

"Where is Thaddeus?" I ignored his comment in hopes of buying time or convincing him to let me go. Either way, I knew at that moment, I wasn't making it out of here the same way that I came in.

His head shook in confusion and annoyance, "This is pointless. I am going to enjoy this," he said as the energy that he wanted caught my breath and threatened to surrender to him. I didn't want him anywhere near me and I wasn't going to give up. I needed to stay in this realm long enough for Thad to find me. *Please find me.*

In slow motion, I fought for enough of myself over the years that I wasn't willing to give it up to a guard in my way from finding Thad. The moment he put his hand on my shoulder, everything changed.

"Ashley," I heard his voice off in the distance.

Dominic's darkness flowed in to me, grounding me. He didn't expect for me to humanize.

With a deep breath, I was going to play his game. He wanted me and I was going to free the others like me from this cold and demonic asshole. He stood with his mouth agape while I smiled. Never had I imagined this would be possible, but it is.

"It's true," he said as I began the draw of power. I wanted him dead.

"What's true?" I still didn't understand.

"Put on the whole armour of God, that ye may be able to stand against the wiles of the devil." The quote was from the bible and referred in regards to my kind. Are we real and do we stand a chance against those of the dark? We are and we do.

Having built the strength to survive the soul transfer, I looked over Dominic's shoulder. Thaddeus quietly moved behind him.

"Good bye, Dominic," I said.

Thaddeus had a glow that resembled the souls that I was trying to save. Thad wouldn't kill one of me, would he?

Dominic's face lost all of its color as Thaddeus's color brightened. His face contorted as he syphoned the life out of Dominic. Thad is strong but is he strong enough to hold all of this energy? Neither of them moved as the battle for power threatened both of their lives.

"Thaddeus, are you okay?" I had to do something, but I was at a loss.

He didn't say a thing. No response was harder than I had expected. I couldn't lose him and here I was watching him give up his life for me. He didn't need to do this and there was nothing that I could do to stop him. I was a ghost for fuck sake.

"Fuck, Thaddeus. I told you to find him, not kill him," Drake said coming to a stop right behind Thad.

"Do something," I pleaded with Drake. I couldn't believe I was asking for help from someone that threatened to end me, but I was desperate,.

"Honey, you are going to have to wait. Until the transfer is done, there is nothing that you can do."

"I have seen him take power before. It is painful and it will kill him."

Drake looked at me with squinted lids, "He is going to die, whether I stop him now or not. The amount of energy he has acquired has never been consumed by a single vampire."

"I just saw Dominic standing in front of me. He held the same power that Thaddeus is fucking with. Don't lie to me, Drake." I was starting to slip in and out of a vision and I fought to avoid the part of my job that I used to enjoy.

Tears began their long journey down my cheeks. I couldn't tell what was making me cry, the fact that I was going to lose him or that there was nothing I could do about it.

Everything began flickering from color to black and white. I couldn't dream now, I had to stay here. I didn't want to see anything other than Thaddeus standing in front of me, free from all of this paranormal bullshit. I wanted him here, with me.

Drake pulled me back to this world, away from whatever void from existence was summoning me, "What you didn't see was Thaddeus just drank down so much energy that it had to be split amongst two vampires. The last Lord that tried to consume it all had combusted, releasing all of you back in to the world. By keeping you with vampires, we were able to keep an eye on the power source and lend some security to both lost souls and vampires." His eyes were the same violet color as Thad's, making me want to break down and give up. I didn't want to live without him in a world full of vampires and darkness.

Dominic fell to the floor, leaving Thaddeus standing with his eyes closed. The energy was too much for him to contain. His entire body shook as the sparks in his aura flashed brighter and more frequent.

"What do I do?" I begged for help from anyone listening. Heaven and Hell both would rue the day they took him from me. I was watching Thad die and they were allowing it.

It will kill you. Whatever he says, don't.

Thaddeus's words wrecked my body with cries of pain. I couldn't do nothing. I would rather die than be alone to wander the earth with someone else.

"I'd rather do hard with you, than easy alone." I said out loud as well as in response to him.

"I know what to do," I said as Thaddeus fell to his knees.

I lowered myself to him, lifting my hands to his face without touching him. It wasn't time yet. His eyes opened as if he sensed me. I could feel the pull from him as I moved closer.

"Hi," I whispered through sobbing tears.

Don't do this.

"I have to."

You will be okay. Please, listen to me this time.

"I can do this without you, but I don't want to."

I can't do this without you.

My heart broke with his silent admission, but I has to be selfish for the first time since I met him.

"I love you," I whispered as I readied for the pain.

My fingertips touched his face gently as I tested the exchange. I could do this, I had to. Unlike a vampire, I was a ghost. "I was made for this. Trust me,"

Before he could respond, the brightest burst of light startled me. I shut my eyes and prepared for the worst.

The constant flow of energy didn't change but my surroundings did.

Virginia Johnson

Chapter Fourteen
Ashley

"Where am I?" I found myself in an ally, caught between a wall and a dumpster. I quickly crawled from my knees, looking for anything that I recognize.

Without warning, the silent pavement shook with bass from a huge speaker. I grabbed my head to avoid losing focus on where I was.

A car swerved down the street, narrowly missing a street light and an accident. The train bells were as loud as the music and the steady beeping. Nothing made sense as I started seeing everything in fast-forward then slow motion. I clamped my hands over my ears and let a scream rip through my throat. A loud bang halted everything as my knees hit the ground.

Waiting for it all to start again, I opened my eyes to a white van parked beside a convenience store, the same convenience store I saw in my vision. I pulled myself from the gravel, running to the other side of the parked barrier, seeing there was no mutilated mess on the wall. There was mumbling coming from behind the sliding of the van. Pulling it open, there was a little girl, bound with ropes and duct tape.

I quickly unbound her hands, leaving her to remove the tape. "Don't tell him you heard me. He was going to bring me snacks and let me go. I don't have to play like dress-up if I was quiet."

"Oh honey, I need you to run. Run as far away from here as you can. Find an adult and tell them to call the police. You are going to be safe if you let me do what I have to, okay? Do you understand, princess?"

Her panicked nod was enough for me. I pointed her in the direction of the fast-food restaurant down the street, "Go there. Hurry."

As she made he escape I waited for the bastard in black to make his way towards me.

***

I blinked, finding myself in a car. I was startled by my new location, but I knew exactly where I was. I was going to prevent him from killing a baby.

The country music played as it did in my vision, causing him to sway to the song. The caramel liquor was flowing down his throat while I hoped he would choke on it.

As if I had pressed play on a video, this vision played out as it did before. This time I was ready for whatever was going to happen. The driver wasn't ready for what was going to happen, but I was ready. The car swerved back and forth over the double yellow lines as cars passed on the left. I watched the road instead of him. His choking caught my attention as he took another swig from the bottle.

Not paying attention to the road I looked up to a yellow bus, loading the smallest of children. They were so small and not ready to leave this world. I looked over to the left, to see a minivan approaching. The minivan.

Without hesitation, I flickered into the car, grabbed the driver and his wife. The small boy in the back seat was playing with the baby locked into the car seat. I grabbed the boy next, delivering him to outside of the vehicle on the side of the road. I struggled with the crying baby boy in the seat, "You need to trust me, little guy. I am going to make sure you live a very long life." After releasing both the car seat and the buckle holding him securely in place, I delivered him to the grassy shoulder behind his loving family.

Returning to the drunk driver, I yanked on the wheel causing him to run head first in to the empty van. Without me, he could've killed a countless number of undeserving children.

***

Smoke and sweat burned my nostrils as the music started pounding through the oversized speakers. Standing off to the side of the stage, I watched a s fans screamed and danced to the melodic vocals from the lead singer. His hips swayed in an inviting manner, causing the girls in the front row to melt to the floor.

A crashing sound caught my attention behind the stage. Following the screams from a distance, I found myself in a long line of women holding a slew of things that they were wanting to have signed by the lead singer heart throb himself.

There was a girl being escorted out the back door, wailing and screaming inaudible words. The music was too loud for me to understand her pleas as she was thrown out of the building like garbage.

As the security guards made their way back towards me, their conversation was one that I could only hope that the girl in the back wasn't a part of. I didn't wait to find out, I hauled ass down the corridor to the exit.

Pushing open the heavy metal, I saw the barely dressed girl rolled in to a ball in a pile of garbage bags. Her pulse was weak but she was responsive. "Hey, wake up, hun."

She moaned in to her elbow before looking up to me, "I said 'no,' but he didn't listen. I didn't want to go backstage. The syringe hurts. I don't remember, but I am bleeding."

I started checking her arms for blood before moving to her neck. She grabbed my hand as I started to move away from her. "I don't see any blood."

"Not here," she lifted her skirt, revealing blood between her legs. "I never wanted it. I told him that, but he told me... I had to, that no-one would believe... that the lead singer of HypeJax... would need to... rape... me."

She lost consciousness as I stood with my own blood boiling. He raped her and I wasn't going to let that go unjustified.

As I walked back in to the venue, I was on a mission that I wouldn't abandon. Halfway down the hall, I saw a door cracked open. Kicking it in, here lay another half-dressed girl with her legs spread but her panties were still intact. That was all it took for me to make sure it never happened again.

Having spent hours on a stage, playing the piano, I knew exactly what to do. I slipped beneath the stage and released the pins holding the center of the stage intact. I heard the drum set jar and the cymbal crash to the floor. I needed to move forward a bit if I was going to stop the rapist from acting again. Kicking out the locking bolts, the stage began buckling.

It was only a matter of time before he would put enough weight on the platform and end himself in the process.

The smell of burning flesh was worse than the drunk driver, and I was ok with it.

***

As the boys were running alongside of the train tracks, I watched from a distance as they waited for the train. I knew they were up to no good, but there was something off about the two hovering over a phone. They were more interested in the message than the racing train approaching them.

"Do it. It will be funny, man," was all I heard before moving closer to the boys.

"Nah, he's not worth it," was all the boy had to say for me to move closer to them.

Their ride was nearly there as one of the boys from the back shouted to them.

Across the screen I saw exactly what was so important.

Danny: Leave me alone or I will do it.

No-one will miss you. End your life and everyone will be happy.

MESSAGE UNDELIVERED

Before he could hit send and without warning, I grabbed the kid by the shirt and pushed him in to the train. Danny wasn't going to be bullied today.

***

There I stood in the woods, surrounded by scurrying animals and falling leaves. There was a truck parked near an opening within the forest. I saw a smoldering piece of paper alongside of the blue 4x4. I stomped on it, extinguishing the flame. There wasn't much I could read, but I saw enough.

To the parents of Sarah Lynn,

The life insurance policy will reflect the changes that you have requested. The amount of $500,000 will be paid to the listed beneficiaries upon death.

As soon as I finished that sentence, my heart dropped. I could hear a little girl counting from the trees and I needed to find her before her parents did.

I grabbed a gun from the front seat of the truck and took off after the little girl. She disappeared through the thick brush, leaving me with little to no time to find her.

I heard the bullet enter the chamber as I came up on the side of the man. I held my arms up and pointed, "Don't do it," I warned.

I saw his finger twitch against the trigger, so I pulled mine. She didn't deserve to die, not at the hands of her own father. "I am so sorry. I didn't…"

"Did you catch it, Daddy?" Sarah came running towards her bleeding father, leaving me with no choice but to keep her safe.

***

The monitors in a hospital tell a thousand stories, finding the right cure can be much more difficult. Standing outside of the hospital room, I saw a nurse slip into the room with her hands in her pocket, facing the ground. Suspicions were high and I needed to know what was going on.

As I peeked through the door, I saw it safe to slip in behind her.

"If only you would be trusted to keep your mouth shut, this wouldn't be a problem. I told you his was our little secret and you chose to use it to black mail me. Unfortunately, with you dead, your father will continue to need me in his life. With you in this state, no one must visit or ask questions." I could hear her confession as if it were rehearsed. "It will be our little secret, until you're dead, of course."

She turned around to face the TV as I slipped under the bed. The nurse pulled the medication from the syringe and inserted it in to the IV. I reached out, pinching off the vile feeding and hoped she would hurry out of the room.

As I had hoped she did, but another set of feet appeared out of nowhere. I watched as she read the chart and walked over to the machines. I couldn't hold the toxic syrup from entering him for long, so I pulled the plug on the stand. The loud beeping was going to bring unwanted attention, so I crawled out of my hiding spot to come face to face with myself. She, I, looked scared. I held my finger to my mouth with a "Shhh…" If she was the me from earlier, she will understand as I did.

Grabbing another bottle from my pocket, I inserted it in to a spare syringe and injected him with the necessary dose. Within minutes the boy came to, as the nurses and doctors filled the room.

He had heard everything the woman had said and began his side of the story. I slipped out during the commotion.

Virginia Johnson

Chapter Fifteen

Ashley

The bright light flickered me back to the stone corridor. I looked around to find myself holding on to Thaddeus as the energy finished the transfer.

"Hello, Ashley," a voice that I recognized welcomed.

"What are you doing here? You turned me away." I said to the decision maker that assigned me to wander the planet as a ghost.

He looked to Thad and I as he continued, "Only a special person could handle the energy disbursement needed to accomplish what you just did."

"What do you mean, disbursement? I am right there, still pulling it from him in attempt to save his life," I screamed. "I killed five people in my visions."

"No, you killed five people that deserved it. We are not to judge the actions of others, but we can save the future of our kind," his cryptic talk was confusing me.

"What are you talking about?"

"Ashley, the only way anyone, including yourself, were to absorb that kind of power would be to use it. Anyone else would have gone crazy with anger and fear, but you did the opposite. You acted out of love," he clarified.

"But I killed five people out of anger," he cut me off before I could continue.

"You did the right thing with the energy that you were given by accomplishing six tasks simultaneously. Your silence, strength and empathy for others controlled the outcome of the situations. You did the right thing with the power that was forced on you. There is a secondary part of you that most others of your kind are not gifted with."

He still didn't make sense, but I was listening. "I couldn't let him die," I said as I turned to Thaddeus.

"Because you love him," he said factually.

"Yes."

"You have earned your place on the other side, and I am here to collect you." He said with sadness in his voice.

"I don't want to go," I whispered.

He looked to me with squinted eyes, "You are being offered a lifetime of peace and you are tuning it down for... this?" he looked around with his palms turned up.

"No, I am turning it down for... him. I will choose him every time."

He bowed his head, looking to the two of us in a tight embrace on the floor, "Then it shall be done."

With another burst of light, I was blown backwards to the floor.

"Ouch," I said as I tried to sit up. If I were a ghost, I shouldn't have felt that. "Being a human, sucks."

I didn't mean to say that out loud, as I hear Drake chuckle from my side.

"I told you she would be fine. She isn't like the other ones, Thaddeus," Drake said as Thad moved closer to my side.

"No, she isn't. She is better than the others," he responded to Drake before he leaned down to talk to me.

"Hey. How ya feeling?" His fingers wrapped in to my hair.

"Fine, I think. Falling hurts more than I remember," I whine.

"There are some downsides to being human, but there are some pretty great things, too."

"I know, I was human. Now, I am... Wait, what am I?" I look around for an answer. "He didn't tell me?"

"Who are you looking for?" he seemed concerned as he checked the back of my head for blood.

"He gave me a choice and disappeared."

"What did you choose?"

"You," I whispered as his forehead met mine.

"I forgot to tell you something, while you were off saving innocents."

"What's that?"

His eyes were a richer shade of violet than I remember, "I love you, too, Ashley"

His lips brushed against mine, leaving me breathless and wanting more. My eyes closed instinctively as he deepened the kiss.

"I'll just be in the Lords chambers until you're done," Drake said as he disappeared down the hallway.

Thaddeus pulled away slightly, "I've missed this. At least we know I can make you real, or something like it, without killing you."

"Take me home, Thaddeus."

The End

Follow Virginia Johnson

Indie Book Network
http://www.indiebooknetwork.com
https://www.facebook.com/indiebooknetwork/

Facebook

https://facebook.com/AuthorVirginiaJohnson/

Twitter

https://twitter.com/AuthorVJohnson

Instagram

https://www.instagram.com/charmedchic24/

Newsletter

http://tinyletter.com/VirginiaLeeJohnson

Website:
AuthorVirginiajohnson.com

Indie book Channel

https://www.facebook.com/TheIndieBookChannel/
https://www.youtube.com/channel/UCeGKDtCb8TpoCounkSKorpg

Fan Group

https://www.facebook.com/groups/KylesHarem/

Tampa

https://www.facebook.com/TampaIndieAuthorBookConvention/

Tampaindieauthorbookconvention.wordpress.com

Made in the USA
Middletown, DE
14 December 2017